Superconductivity

Superconductivity

From Discovery to Breakthrough

Charlene W. Billings

Illustrated with photographs and diagrams

COBBLEHILL BOOKS/DUTTON

New York

In memory of
Barry's mother and father

Library of Congress Cataloging-in-Publication Data
Billings, Charlene W.
Superconductivity : from discovery to breakthrough / Charlene
W. Billings : illustrated with photographs and diagrams.
p.   cm.
Includes index.
Summary: Discusses the development of new and different types of
materials intended to conduct energy more efficiently and how they may be used.
ISBN 0-525-65048-2.   1. Superconductivity—Juvenile literature.   [1. Superconductors.
2. Superconductivity.]   I. Title.
QC611.922.B55 1991 537.6'23—dc20 90-20782 CIP AC

Published in the United States by
Cobblehill Books, an affiliate of Dutton Children's Books,
a division of Penguin Books USA Inc.
Designer: Jean Krulis
Printed in Hong Kong First Edition
10 9 8 7 6 5 4 3 2 1

Contents

1

What Is Superconductivity?

A Dutch scientist in Leiden named Heike Kamerlingh Onnes was doing experiments in 1911 to learn how metals are affected by very cold temperatures. While he was working with the metal mercury, he discovered something important that no one else before had ever known. When mercury is cooled to the extremely low temperature of liquid helium, it suddenly allows electricity to flow through it without any loss of energy.

Onnes and other scientists investigated other metals to learn if they would act the same way and found that many did. One experiment Onnes did was to form a metal wire loop and cool it in liquid helium. He started a flow of electricity in the wire circuit and then removed the source of electricity. If the ring of wire had not been cooled in liquid helium, the electric current immediately would have been lost. But one year later, kept at the supercool temperature of liquid helium,

an electric current of the original strength was still flowing in the metal ring!

Onnes was not able to explain what he had discovered, but he called the phenomenon *superconductivity*.

INSULATORS TO SUPERCONDUCTORS

Electricity is the flow of electrons through a material. And a material that allows electricity to flow through it is a *conductor*. One of the best conductors of electricity is the metal copper. For this reason copper is used in the transmission lines that carry electricity from power plants to schools, factories, and homes. The appliances and lamps in our homes also have copper wires.

There are other materials that do not allow electricity to flow through them. They are *insulators*. Glass, wood, and rubber are examples of good insulators. The copper wires of appliances in your home are covered with an insulating coating so that you will not get an electrical shock when you touch them.

A third group of materials allows some electricity to flow, but not as well as true conductors. These materials are somewhere in between conductors and insulators and are called *semiconductors*. An example of a semiconductor is silicon, which is specially treated to make microchips for computers.

Though copper is an excellent conductor, some of the energy in the current that flows through it is lost. As electric current passes through copper wire, some electrons collide with atoms in their path, other electrons, or impurities in the metal. In these collisions, some of the

Portrait of H.K. Onnes

electrons' energy is turned into heat instead of electrical energy. The opposition against the free flow of electrons in a conductor is called *resistance*.

Conductors, semiconductors, insulators, and superconductors can be compared. Conductors have little resistance, semiconductors have some resistance, and insulators have very high resistance. The importance of superconductors is that they show *no* resistance to the flow of electricity when cooled to the correct temperature.

But what is the "correct" temperature and how do we measure it?

MEASURING TEMPERATURE

In the United States, most of the thermometers we see that measure air temperature use the *Fahrenheit scale*. This temperature scale is named after a Dutch scientist Gabriel Daniel Fahrenheit, who invented the first mercury thermometer around 1714.

Fahrenheit's thermometer consisted of a hollow glass tube with a bulb full of liquid mercury at the base. The slim shaft of empty space in the hollow tube above the mercury contained nothing, not even air. When the mercury in the bulb was heated, it was forced to rise in a column in the hollow space. If the mercury was then cooled, the column fell.

The next step in making a thermometer was to mark the glass column with divisions. Fahrenheit called each division a *degree*. He then labeled the freezing point of salt water as zero on his thermometer's scale. Next he marked the freezing point and the boiling point of pure water. Using Fahrenheit's scale, the freezing point of pure water is 32° Fahrenheit or 32° F. And the boiling point of pure water is 212° F.

Scientists and much of the rest of the world use a simpler scale to measure temperature. About 1742, a Swedish astronomer, Anders Celsius, made a mercury thermometer with a scale that had 100 divisions or degrees between the freezing point and the boiling point of pure water. The freezing point of water on the *Celsius scale* is read as 0° Celsius or 0° C and the boiling point as 100° Celsius or 100° C. This scale is easier to use, so it has become popular throughout most of the world.

HOW COLD IS COLD?

In the universe and in nature, temperatures can be much higher than the boiling point of water and much lower than the freezing point of water. For example, the interior temperature of our Sun may be as high as 15,000,000° C (27,000,000° F). And in the outer reaches of our solar system, the planet Pluto may have temperatures as low as -218° C (-360° F).

Just how cold can things get? Many scientists wondered about this question and tried to find the answer.

By the mid-1800s many scientists, including British scientist William Thomson, believed that all substances were made of atoms. Two or more atoms usually combine to form a *molecule*. The molecules in gases can move about freely. In liquids and solids, the motion of the molecules is less free, but they can move back and forth in place or vibrate. This motion shows that the molecules have energy.

As the temperature of a substance is raised, the molecules contain more energy and they move about more rapidly. As the temperature of a substance is lowered, the molecules in it contain less energy and move about more slowly.

Thomson, who is more popularly known as Lord Kelvin, reasoned that if the temperature dropped low enough, the molecules would stop moving and would contain no energy. This temperature is known as *absolute zero* and is at -273.15° C.

Lord Kelvin measured all temperatures from absolute zero upward in Celsius degrees. His temperature scale is the *absolute* or *Kelvin scale*. Absolute zero is 273.15 degrees below the freezing point of water. On the Celsius scale water boils at 100° C, so on the Kelvin scale, water boils at 100° + 273.15° or 373.15° Kelvin or 373.15° K.

The low temperatures used to study superconductivity are usually measured on the Kelvin scale. For example, helium gas becomes a liquid at 4.2° K (-268.9° C).

COMPARISON OF TEMPERATURE SCALES

	Fahrenheit	Celsius	Kelvin
Water freezes	32°	0°	273°
Water boils	212°	100°	373.15°
Room temperature	68°	20°	293°
Body temperature	98.6°	37°	310°
Absolute zero	-459.4°	-273°	0°
Liquid helium	-451.8°	-268.9°	4.2°
Liquid nitrogen	-320.8°	-196°	77°

Although Onnes discovered superconductivity in 1911, it was many years before the great potential of his discovery could be used in practical ways. Liquid helium and the equipment needed to cool superconducting materials to temperatures near 4° K are too expensive and difficult to handle to be used routinely outside scientific laboratories.

2

The Superconductivity
Race Heats Up

Scientists in many parts of the world continued to work with different materials, seeking superconductors that would operate at higher temperatures than 4° K. By 1933, some combinations of metals known as *alloys* were found to be superconductors at 10° K. Still, this temperature was too cold to be of practical use.

The temperature needed for superconductivity to occur is called the *critical temperature*, T_c. A jump in the critical temperature occurred in 1969 when 20° K was reached. Then in 1973, the critical temperature for superconductivity to occur was raised again to 23° K. But no further success in improving the T_c was achieved for another thirteen years.

FIRST BREAKTHROUGH

Two researchers at the International Business Machines (IBM) laboratories in Zurich, Switzerland, K. Alex Müller and J. Georg

IBM researchers K. Alexander Müller and J. George Bednorz

Bednorz, tried working with new kinds of *ceramic* materials. Ceramics are usually thought of as insulators, but some of them have features similar to metals. These ceramics are called *perovskites*.

For three years the two IBM researchers tirelessly tried to reach higher temperatures for superconductivity by testing hundreds of different samples of perovskites. Finally, in 1986, after many discouraging failures, they succeeded in reaching a critical temperature of 30° K. The superconductor they discovered was a ceramic oxide of the metals barium, lanthanum, and copper.

Müller and Bednorz published an historic paper describing their work in September, 1986. And in 1987, these two researchers were awarded the Nobel Prize for their discovery.

The temperature breakthrough announced in Müller's and Bednorz's paper ignited a renewed interest in superconductivity all over the world. An area of scientific research that had been dormant for years suddenly came to life. By November, 1986, many groups of scientists at locations dotted around the world were working feverishly to raise the critical temperature at which superconductivity would occur.

RACE TO THE MAGIC MARK

One group of scientists was led by Dr. Ching-Wu Paul Chu at the University of Houston in Texas. Dr. Maw-Kuen Wu of the University of Alabama at Huntsville worked in collaboration with Dr. Chu. Another group was under the direction of Shoji Tanaka at the University of Tokyo in Japan. And an additional group consisted of Robert J. Cava, Robert B. von Dover, Bertram Batlogg, and Edward A. Ritman working at Bell Laboratories in Murray Hill, New Jersey. Scientists in China also did superconductivity research.

These groups of scientists competed with each other, working day and night, toward higher and higher critical temperatures for superconductivity. Within weeks, the T_c reached 40° K. Then, the T_c jumped to over 50° K.

All of these researchers were in a heated race, moving toward what

Portrait of Müller, Chu, and Tanaka at March 18, 1987, meeting called the "Woodstock of Physics"

they called the "magic" 77° K mark. For if superconductivity could be achieved at a temperature of 77° K or above, a truly significant threshold would have been crossed.

At temperatures above 77° K, liquid nitrogen, which is less expensive than liquid helium, could be used as a cooling agent for superconductivity. The air surrounding the Earth is about 80 percent nitrogen, so the supply is unlimited. And liquid nitrogen can easily be carried around in a Thermos. Liquid helium, on the other hand, requires bulky, inconvenient cooling equipment and costs at least six times as much as liquid nitrogen.

90° K AND BEYOND

At last, on January 29, 1987, Dr. Paul Chu in cooperation with Dr. Maw-Kuen Wu broke through the "magic" temperature barrier. He and his co-workers reported finding superconductivity at temperatures over 90° K! The material they had used to accomplish this feat was an oxide of the metals yttrium, barium, and copper.

On Wednesday, March 18, 1987, physicists from all over the world met at the Hilton Hotel in New York City to learn about the latest

Photograph of standing-room-only crowd at meeting called the "Woodstock of Physics"

discoveries in superconductivity research. As each scientist spoke and revealed a new advance, the standing-room-only audience of normally self-controlled physicists cheered as if at a rock concert. The event is now referred to as the "Woodstock of Physics," and was a celebration of scientific achievement.

During the spring of 1987, two researchers at the University of Arkansas joined the rush to look for new superconductors. Dr. Allen Hermann and his associate Zhengzhi Sheng decided to try an oxide of the metals thallium, barium, and copper. On February 22, 1988, they presented data to the World Congress on Superconductivity in Houston that showed zero resistance in two samples of their thallium compound at 106° K.

During the International Conference on High Temperature Superconductors held in Interlaken from February 29 through March 4, 1988, Dr. Paul Grant of IBM reported that the IBM group at Almaden, California, had prepared samples of thallium compound that showed superconductivity at the critical temperature of 125° K.

The first United States patent in high-temperature superconductivity was awarded to IBM for their 125° K thallium superconductor.

Some scientists are concerned about working with thallium because it is one of the most poisonous elements. However, thallium is not as dangerous once it is made into a superconductor. By comparison, the oxides of lead, nickel, and cadmium, among others, are considered more poisonous than thallium.

Thousands of scientists all over the world are still working hard to find new materials with higher critical temperatures for superconductivity. In time, it is hoped that a superconductor that will operate at room temperature will be discovered. At this temperature, no cooling agent would be needed for superconductivity to occur.

3

What Do We Know About Superconductors?

Each element is composed of one kind of atom, and all of the elements have been organized into a chart known as the *periodic table*. Each element on the periodic table has a symbol that identifies it. For example, the metal tin has the symbol Sn and the gas oxygen has the symbol O. (Some of the symbols are taken from the Latin names for the elements. The symbol for tin, Sn, comes from the Latin word for tin, *stannum*.) Similar elements are grouped together on the periodic table. Thus, metals that share some characteristics are positioned close to each other on the table.

Two or more atoms can combine to form a molecule. For example, an atom of tin can combine with an atom of oxygen to form a molecule of tin oxide. The symbol for tin oxide is SnO.

THE STRUCTURE OF A SUPERCONDUCTOR

The atoms of a superconductor are bound together in a three-

A single crystal of high-temperature, superconducting material, yttrium-barium-copper oxide

dimensional, gridlike, repeating pattern. The arrangement is characteristic of a *crystal* and known as a *lattice structure*. The lattice structure is like a framework that holds individual atoms in specific positions.

The superconductor discovered by Dr. Paul Chu at the University of Houston has a critical temperature of at least 90° K. It has a lattice structure containing atoms of oxygen and of the metals yttrium, barium, and copper.

A scientist would write the chemical symbols $YBa_2Cu_3O_7$ to stand for the atoms in this superconductor. The numbers tell the scientist how many atoms of each element are in each molecule of the substance. $YBa_2Cu_3O_7$ stands for one atom of yttrium, two atoms of barium, three atoms of copper, and seven atoms of oxygen in one molecule of this superconductor.

Picture the lattice structure of $YBa_2Cu_3O_7$ as a stack of three cubes, each with a metal atom at its center. The cube at the bottom of the pile has barium at its center and the one above it has ytrrium at its center. The top cube has barium at its center again. Copper atoms are located at the corners of each of the three cubes with oxygen atoms between them.

FEATURES OF SUPERCONDUCTORS

A unique characteristic of the structure of $YBa_2Cu_3O_7$ is that the atoms of copper and oxygen are arranged in layers or planes. Thus far, all of the known high-temperature superconductors have this special feature.

Another characteristic of superconductors is that they can repel or keep out a magnetic field. This unusual phenomenon was discovered in 1933 and is known as the *Meissner effect*.

21

Model of yttrium-barium-copper oxide is held by chemist Donald Murray.

Computer-generated image of crystal structure of high-temperature superconducting material. Yttrium atoms are shown as silver, barium green, copper blue, and oxygen red.

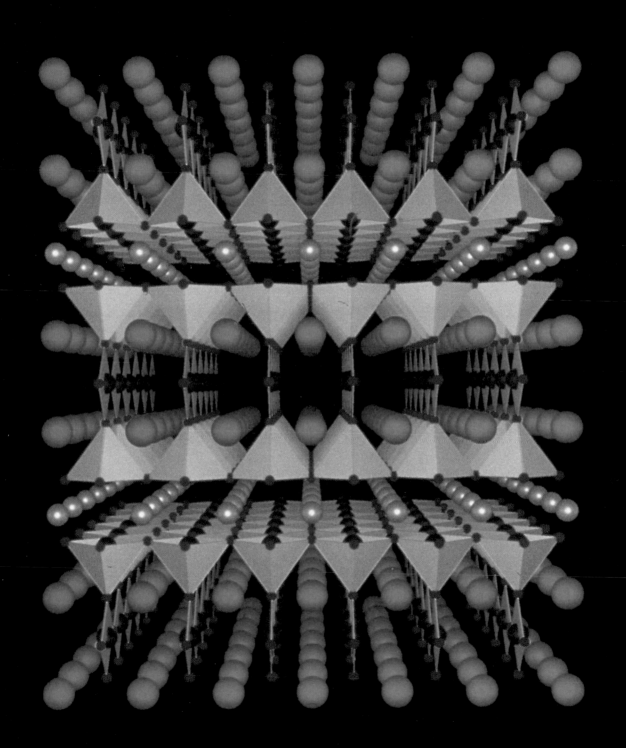

The Meissner effect can be demonstrated by placing a magnet on a superconductor pellet and then pouring a bath of liquid nitrogen around the base of the pellet. As long as the pellet is superconducting, the magnet will appear to float above the superconductor. This is one of the ways scientists test materials for superconductivity.

There are two types of superconductors. Type I superconductors are metals such as mercury, tin, and lead in which superconductivity was first observed. Type I superconductors repel a magnetic field until the field reaches a strength called the *critical field*. Beyond this point, the superconductor loses its ability to conduct electricity without resistance.

Type II superconductors are materials like alloys or metallic oxides that have two critical fields. These superconductors continue to conduct electricity without resistance until the magnetic field becomes strong enough to go beyond the second critical field. Only then is their ability to superconduct an electric current lost.

In addition to being defeated by a large magnetic field, superconductivity may also be destroyed when an electrical current that is too great is passed through a superconductor. The size of the current that can pass through a superconductor without loss of its ability to superconduct is called the *critical current*.

THEORIES ABOUT SUPERCONDUCTORS

There are several theories which try to explain superconductivity. One of these is known as the *BCS theory*. It is named after the three

Demonstration of the Meissner effect

Portrait of Bardeen, Cooper, and Schrieffer

scientists who devised it—John Bardeen, Leon Cooper, and J. R. Schrieffer. These researchers shared the Nobel Prize in 1972 for their work.

As individual electrons travel through an ordinary conductor, some of them collide with each other or with other atoms. They can be compared to a crowd of people jostled together and out of step with each other. When electrons collide, some of their energy is lost in the form of heat.

The BCS theory states that during superconductivity electrons pair up as they flow through the lattice structure of the superconductor. As they travel, the paired electrons, called *Cooper Pairs*, clear a collision-free pathway for other electrons. The movement of the paired electrons can be compared to a large group of people locking arms and marching in step.

According to the BCS theory, superconductivity is lost above the critical temperature because, as warming occurs, the atoms in the lattice start to vibrate too much. This increased atomic motion splits apart the electron pairs and the collision-free pathway for other electrons vanishes.

The BCS theory seems to explain superconductivity for the low-temperature superconducting materials such as mercury, tin, and lead. However, it was devised before the more recently discovered high-temperature superconductors were known.

A theory is needed to account for superconductivity in the high-temperature superconductors. As more research is done with the newer superconductors, scientists will be able to better understand superconductivity in these materials and to devise a theory to explain it.

4

Uses for
Superconductivity

There are many potential uses for superconductivity. Among those that hold promise are electronic devices, medical applications, improvements in providing electric power, communications, transportation, military uses, and scientific research.

ELECTRONIC DEVICES

Superconductors can be used in electronic devices. Computers may change greatly in size and speed in the coming years.

Early computers were built with thousands of vacuum tubes that were about the size of slim light bulbs. The second generation of computers was built with transistors. Transistors made possible much smaller computers because they took far less space and generated far less heat than vacuum tubes. And the third generation of computers was built with integrated circuits which were still smaller than transistors and generated even less heat. Each of these improvements led to smaller and faster computers.

When microchips were devised, the electrical circuitry for computers was miniaturized still further. A single microchip is tiny enough to fit through the eye of a sewing needle. The circuits on a microchip are etched onto a thin film that coats a sliver of silicon. This advance reduced the size and increased the speed of computers once more.

Superconductors may affect future computers as much as the

Close-up of a ceramic substrate patterned with high-temperature superconducting wires using a new IBM plasma spraying technique. Such wires might be used to connect logic and memory chips in computers.

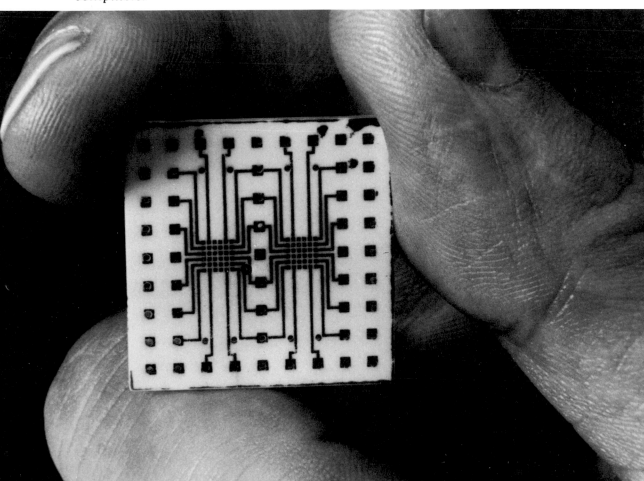

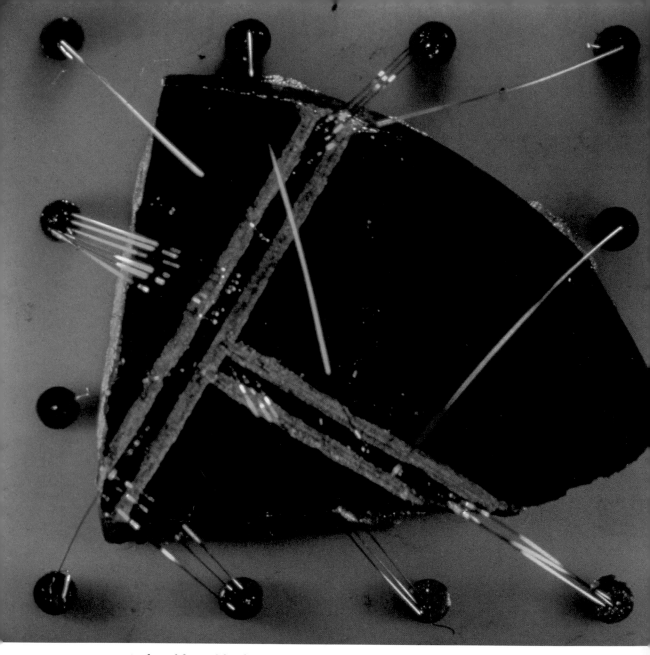

A thin film of high-temperature superconducting material grown on strontium titanate, used in an IBM demonstration that the number of amperes per square centimeter is 100 times greater than previously measured.

inventions of the transistor, the integrated circuit, and the microchip did in the past. If superconductors are used to interconnect modules of integrated circuits inside a computer, the speed with which the computer operates could be increased.

Recently, researchers at International Business Machines produced a *thin film* of superconducting material on a base of strontium titanate. A heated vapor of chemicals is deposited onto a backing material to produce the thin film. The gossamer thin layer of superconducting material is only about one one-hundredth the thickness of a human hair.

When cooled in liquid nitrogen, the thin film carries over 100,000 amperes per square centimeter. An *ampere* is the unit used to measure the strength of an electrical current. This feat is an important step toward finding new applications for superconductors in computers and electronic devices.

More recently, some laboratories made thin films that can carry one million amperes per square centimeter. New ways of applying thin films are being sought, such as attaching them to a backing material that could be wound like a roll of paper towels into a conductor able to carry large electrical currents.

JOSEPHSON JUNCTIONS AND SQUIDS

A *Josephson junction* consists of a thin insulating layer of material sandwiched between two superconductors. Electrons can tunnel through the insulating layer to produce an electrical current.

Josephson junctions can operate as extremely fast switches with a switching speed of less than two picoseconds (a picosecond is one trillionth of a second). For this reason, much research has been done

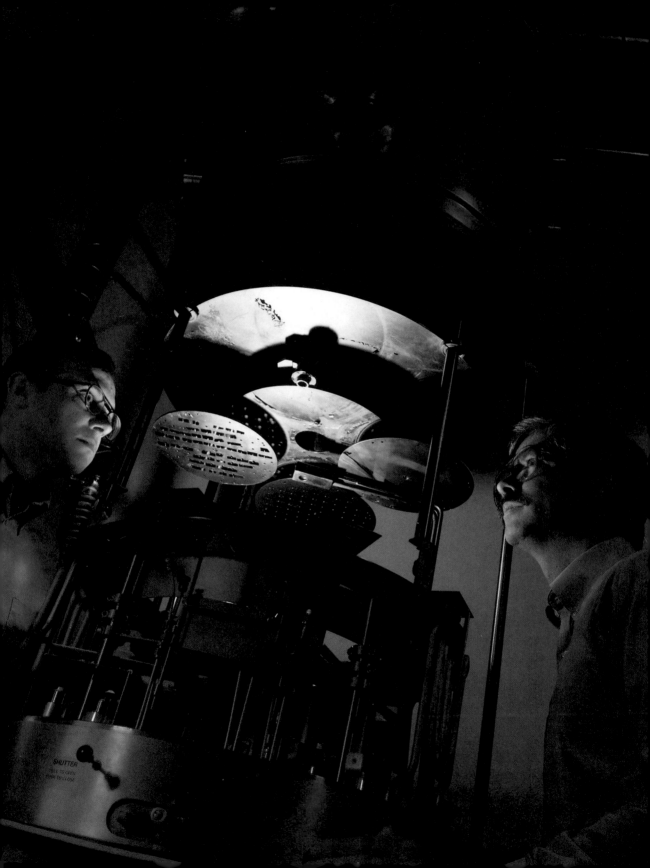

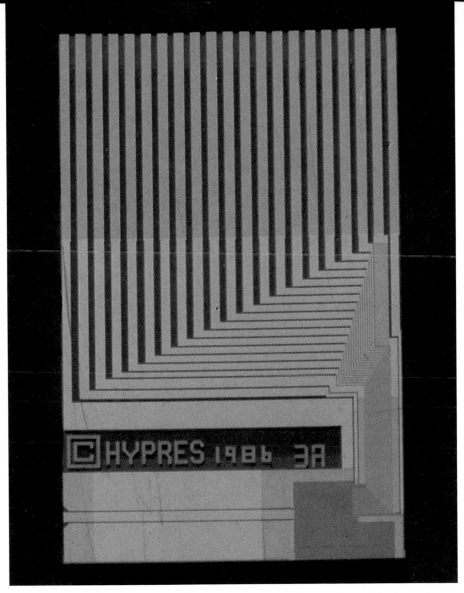

A close-up of a superconducting integrated circuit with Josephson junctions

Dr. Antonio Mogros-Campero (left) and Larry G. Turner ready apparatus for an experiment in which superconducting films are applied to substrates of silicon, the material from which nearly all microchips are made.

Superconducting SQUIDS

to learn if Josephson junctions could be used to create faster computers and communications systems. But because Josephson junctions are very difficult to isolate from one another electrically, other devices may prove to be as advantageous and easier to manufacture.

Another use for Josephson junctions is in the manufacture of extremely sensitive detectors. An invention that uses Josephson junctions in this way is called the Superconducting Quantum Interference Device or SQUID. A SQUID is made of two Josephson junctions coupled together. Because it is a very sensitive instrument for detecting and measuring magnetic fields, another name for a SQUID is a *magnetometer*.

Geologists use SQUIDs to locate subterranean mineral deposits deep within the earth. And the U.S. Navy uses supersensitive SQUIDs to detect submarines and mines in the ocean.

SQUIDs also can be used to detect the faint magnetic fields produced by the tiny electrical currents of the human brain. Physicians can use these devices to evaluate abnormal conditions of the brain to help patients with epilepsy, stroke, or depression.

MAGNETIC RESONANCE IMAGING

Another way in which superconductors are being used in medicine is known as Magnetic Resonance Imaging (MRI). This method of viewing inside the human body may be the most important discovery since the invention of the X ray. Like an X ray, an image made with MRI shows a physician a portion of the inside of the human body. But the details that can be seen using MRI are clearer than ever before possible.

In hospitals where an MRI system has been installed, the need for surgery to find out what is wrong with a patient has been reduced by one-half. Also, MRI shows a clearer picture of the soft tissues of the body, does not expose the patient to radiation, and eliminates the need to inject dyes.

An MRI system has at its heart a large, five-ton superconducting magnet that produces magnetic fields by passing an electrical current through supercooled coils of wire. The coils are cooled to near absolute zero with liquid helium.

Scientists from the U.S. Department of Agriculture (USDA) are

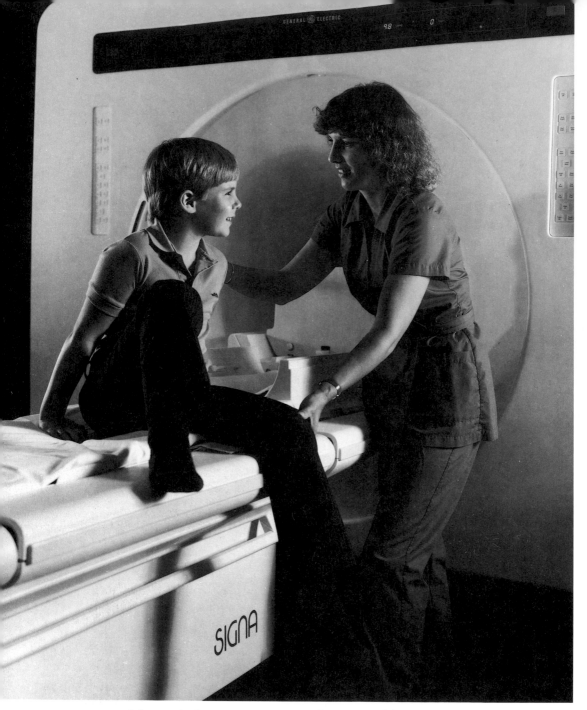

Magnetic Resonance system being used by a young boy and an MR technician

dth= 216 Level=1159
D: 00005
R: 02/04
G: 001/001

R   0 MM

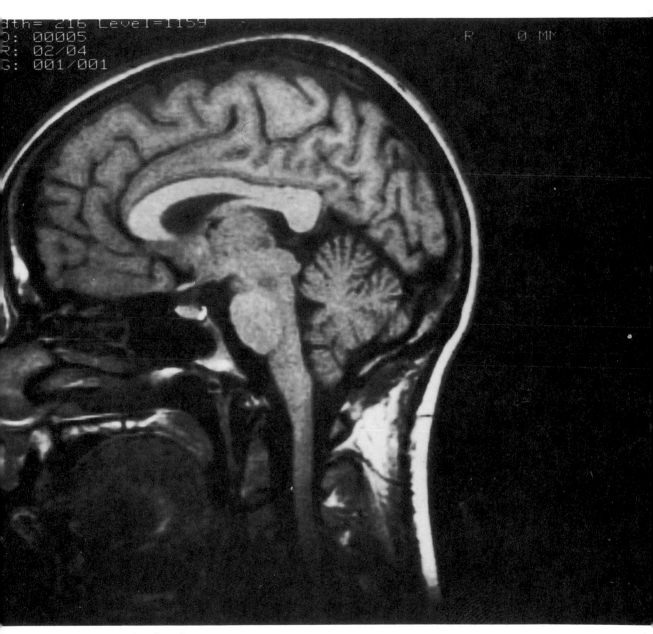

Image of a head using MR system

*Dr. Hugo Rogers (left), a plant physiologist, and Dr. Paul Bottomley,
a physicist, using a Magnetic Resonance scanner to study plants*

working with researchers from General Electric Company using MRI
to study plant growth. MRI allows the scientists to actually watch
plant roots grow in soil without disturbing the plant in any way.

The image of a five-week-old bean seedling produced with MR scanner

TRANSMISSION OF POWER

Commercial superconducting transmission of power was demonstrated in a test in 1982 when 2,000 megawatts of power were transmitted over a cable within a pipe sixteen inches in diameter. Inside the pipe, insulation surrounded the superconductors which were bathed in liquid helium.

The test showed that it may be possible to transmit large quantities of power for distances up to fifty miles. If liquid nitrogen could be used to cool the superconductors, it may be possible to transmit electricity over hundreds of miles. The electricity would be transmitted to its destination through a single supercooled cable.

Superconducting transmission lines may be economical in developing countries where large investment has not been made in an existing power network, as in the United States.

STORAGE OF POWER

Another possible way of using superconductivity in the electric utility industry is in the storage of electricity. During the daytime when people are active, they use large amounts of electricity, putting big demands on the plants that generate the power. However, at night when most people are asleep, power usage is much lower.

In the future, superconducting magnetic energy storage (SMES) systems may be used to store extra electrical current that is produced during periods of low demand. Just as H. K. Onnes "stored" an electrical current in a superconductor circuit for a year, the SMES uses large superconducting coils housed underground to store electricity until it is needed.

Superconducting electrical power generators may be only half the

A superconducting electric generator tested at GE's Large Steam Turbine-Generator Division. It produces approximately twice as much electricity as could be produced by a conventional generator of comparable size.

size of regular power generators. Their smaller size would mean lower cost to build the generators and the buildings needed to produce electrical power.

NUCLEAR FUSION

In the future, nuclear fusion may be used to produce electric power. During nuclear fusion, lightweight atoms fuse or join together. Energy is released in the process. The energy we receive from our Sun is the result of fusion. And the explosive power of a hydrogen bomb is from an uncontained fusion reaction.

In order to use fusion as an energy source, the fusion reaction must be controlled. The Russians were first to operate a fusion device using superconducting electromagnetic coils to contain the reaction. The donut-shaped systems developed by Russian scientists are called *tokamaks*, which means "strong current."

In the United States, a Large Coil Test Facility using superconducting coils for *tokamaks* is being constructed at Oak Ridge National Laboratory. This facility is designed with six superconducting coils. Three are from the United States and three are from other countries.

COMMUNICATIONS

Improved devices for satellite and communications systems may soon be on the market. Receivers and transmitters using high-temperature superconductors will be able to operate with less interference and with a larger number of channels. Relay stations for cellular telephones may be one of the areas to benefit because they will be able to process more cells.

MAGNETIC SEPARATORS

Another use for superconductors is in *magnetic separators*. Materials that need to be separated are mixed with a magnetic fluid.

The mixture is poured into the top of a superconducting magnetic separator, a tubelike, rotating device. The tube is surrounded by a superconducting electromagnetic coil.

The powerful magnetic field from the separator's magnetic coil attracts the more dense particles in the mixture to move toward the outside of the tube. The less dense particles accumulate near the center. As the particles within the tube move toward the bottom of the separator, the more dense particles near the outside of the device are funneled into one container and the less dense particles near the center into another container.

The first application of a superconducting magnetic separator was in 1986 at the J. M. Huber Corporation's clay processing plant.

MASS DRIVERS

In the future a new way to launch objects, possibly from Earth into space, will be a *mass driver*. A bucketlike magnetic container is rapidly accelerated down a track by superconducting electromagnets. Suddenly the container is stopped. But the payload continues to move and is launched toward its destination.

TRANSPORTATION

Another area that could be affected greatly by superconductors is transportation. In the 1960s a scientist at Massachusetts Institute of Technology, Henry Kolm, had an idea for a train that would be capable of speeds up to 300 miles per hour. Kolm suggested a train that would fly along a frictionless track supported by a powerful magnetic field. Today we call this kind of train a *maglev* train. Maglev stands for "magnetically levitated."

A superconducting magnetic separator in use at the Huber Corporation, Macon, Georgia

In 1987, the Japanese demonstrated a prototype maglev train called MLU-002. The train can travel at over 300 miles per hour. Rubber wheels that can be retracted like landing gear support the train until it is moving fast enough to lift off the track. The train then flies about four inches above the track. The chief researcher working on the Japanese maglev train hopes people will be able to travel from Tokyo to Osaka, a distance greater than 300 miles, in only one hour by the year 2000.

In the United States, maglev trains are being considered as a way to relieve traffic congestion. A two-way train traveling on one fifty-foot right-of-way would be capable of carrying the same number of passengers as about ten lanes of highway traffic at full capacity. A maglev train would use about one-half the energy of the automobiles needed in its place and only about one-quarter the energy of airplanes that transport the same number of passengers.

The major costs of a maglev train are not the superconducting magnets that would be needed by such a transportation system, but purchasing the right-of-way and building and maintaining the precision track necessary for this form of very high-speed travel.

A study done by the Rand Corporation of Santa Monica, California, found that an underground maglev system could be constructed in which the trains would travel in evacuated tunnels. Air in the tunnels would be removed to reduce air resistance. The maglev trains could travel in these tunnels at speeds up to 9,000 miles per hour! This futuristic train would make possible a coast-to-coast trip in the United States in less than an hour.

In another area of transportation, a superconducting electric engine built from low-temperature materials has been tested on a small prototype ship in Japan. In the *magship*, superconducting

magnets arranged along the hull send a powerful magnetic field into the surrounding seawater.

Seawater is a good conductor of electricity because it contains dissolved salts. A generator on the ship sends an electric current into the water at right angles to the magnetic field, creating an electromagnetic force that pushes against the seawater and thrusts the ship forward.

MILITARY USES

The Department of Defense in the United States is supporting research on high-temperature superconductors. There are many possible military applications for this new technology.

Electric motors using superconductors would be simpler in design and have fewer moving parts than those now in use. For these reasons, they probably would need fewer repairs. They also would be much quieter, making submarine detection by an enemy more difficult.

Superconductive electric motors also would be smaller than motors now in use. The saved space could then be used for additional weapons or equipment. This would be especially helpful in the limited quarters on submarines.

Among the most important items for military defense are sensors. These can be located on satellites, ships, submarines, airplanes, in the ocean, and on land. Superconductors make possible more powerful sensors capable of operating over greater distances.

A superconducting levitating train

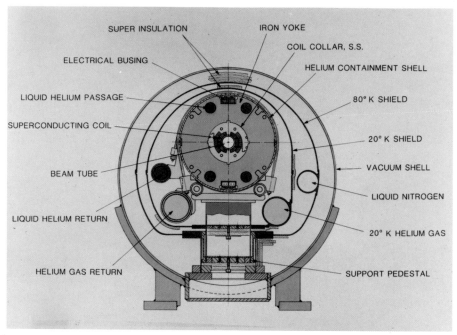

Diagram of a cross-section of a superconducting supercollider magnet

THE SUPERCONDUCTING SUPERCOLLIDER

A scientific application of superconductivity is in the study of the most basic particles of matter. From these studies, researchers are learning new things about matter and about the very beginnings of our universe.

To investigate theories about matter and our universe, scientists use powerful machines called *particle accelerators* or *colliders*. These

Cross-section of a supercollider magnet

48

circular machines use superconducting magnets to accelerate electrically charged particles such as electrons and protons and smash them into other particles. Then the researchers carefully study the interactions of the particles to learn more about them and the forces that control them.

In the United States there is the Tevatron accelerator located at the Fermi National Laboratory in Illinois. The Tevatron was completed in 1983 and is a ring-shaped collider with a particle pathway three and one-half miles long. There are about one thousand superconducting magnets in the Tevatron. They are made of an alloy of niobium and titanium and are cooled using liquid helium.

Now the United States is planning the world's most powerful particle accelerator. It is known as the Superconducting Super Collider or SSC. This giant collider will be twenty times more powerful than the Tevatron and will cost over $4 billion to build. Its construction was authorized by President Ronald Reagan in January of 1987.

When the SSC is built in Waxahachie, Texas, it will use over 10,000 low-temperature superconducting magnets. The ring-shaped pathway that accelerating particles will follow in the SSC will be about fifty-three miles long.

Two beams of protons will be propelled to nearly the speed of light in opposite directions around the circular ring. The protons will be steered to a head-on collision that will recreate conditions that existed in the first split-second of the creation of the universe.

From this research, scientists hope to formulate a single, unifying law of the universe. They hope this one underlying law will explain all of the known theories that we now have about space, time, matter, and energy. Such a unifying law was the lifelong dream of this century's best-known scientist, Albert Einstein.

5

How Are
Superconductors Made?

The high-temperature superconductors are being used mainly in laboratories for research. However, even junior high and high school students have found that under the supervision of their teachers and with the proper precautions they can make high-temperature superconductors in their school laboratories.

An article in the April, 1988, issue of *The Science Teacher* tells how students can make their own superconducting pellets. Also in April, 1988, the National Science Foundation distributed an activity guide to teachers in all United States middle and high schools. The guide describes superconductivity and gives instructions on how to make a superconductor.

On May 22, 1987, Heidi Grant, a fifteen-year-old, eighth-grade student from Dartmouth Middle School, San Jose, California, demonstrated superconductivity to the National Science Board of the National Science Foundation in Washington, D.C. She made the superconductor pellets she used for the demonstration in her father's laboratory at International Business Machines.

Heidi Grant levitating magnet at the NSF, Washington, D.C.

Heidi's father is a research scientist at IBM working on superconductivity. He wanted to prove that high school students could make their own high-temperature superconductors. He located chemistry teacher David Pribyl at Gilroy High School, Gilroy, California, to take on the challenge.

SHAKE AND BAKE

David Pribyl selected his top nine students to attempt to make their own high-temperature superconductors in their high school laboratory. They followed the same procedure as Heidi Grant, sometimes referred to as the "shake-and-bake" method.

As a note of caution, the shake-and-bake method requires working with the oxides of barium and copper, which can be toxic if breathed in or swallowed. *Making a superconductor should only be attempted under the supervision of a teacher and in a laboratory that has proper safety equipment.* It is necessary to wear a dust mask and safety glasses and to grind the ingredients inside a chemical hood.

The metallic oxides of yttrium (Y), barium (Ba), and copper (Cu) are combined so that there is one part yttrium to two parts barium to three parts copper in the mixture. (It is easy to see why this new superconductor is nicknamed the 1-2-3 superconductor.) The metallic oxides are powders that can be weighed on a scale to get the proper proportions.

After weighing the chemicals, the oxides are ground together by hand in a mortar with a pestle until well mixed, usually for about five to ten minutes. (A mortar is a strong porcelain bowl and a pestle is a thick stirrer with a club-shaped end that can be used to crush and mix materials.) The mixture resembles a fine, pale gray powder.

The mixture of powders is baked in a furnace at 950° C in the presence of air for twelve hours. The art departments of some schools have kilns to fire pottery that reach temperatures this high. During this process, the elements in the mixed powders combine chemically to form the new 1-2-3 superconductor. The black material is allowed to cool gradually over a period of five or six hours.

Now the powder must be ground again and formed into pellets with a pellet press. Students sometimes have borrowed a hydraulic press from their school's machine shop or a pill press, such as is used in a pharmacy.

The pellets are baked again at 950° C for twelve hours. If possible, the pellets should be in flowing oxygen. This time, the pellets must be cooled very carefully so that the temperature drops only about 100° C each hour. During this critical cooling period, the pellets take up the oxygen they need to be good superconductors.

TESTING FOR SUPERCONDUCTIVITY

To test for superconductivity, a meter that measures electrical resistance is connected to the pellet. The pellet is place in a bath of liquid nitrogen at 77° K. If no resistance can be detected, the pellet probably is superconducting. However, to demonstrate more conclusively that a material is a superconductor, a test for magnetic levitation also is needed.

The superconductor pellet is put into the cutoff bottom of a styrofoam cup and a samarium-cobalt magnet that is only one-third the size of the pellet is placed on top of the pellet. Using safety glasses and gloves, liquid nitrogen is carefully poured into the cup to surround, but not submerge, the pellet. (Liquid nitrogen is extremely cold and must not touch skin. It can give serious frostbite.)

Within a few seconds, the magnet should levitate and float freely above the superconductor pellet. When one of the students at Gilroy High School finally had success after three tries, she was so excited that she jumped four feet into the air.

PROGRESS AND CHALLENGES AHEAD

Industrial superconductors are manufactured from alloys of the metals niobium and titanium or from compounds of vanadium and gallium. The industrial superconductors can easily be drawn into wires, cables, tapes, and other shapes.

One of the challenges of the newer, high-temperature superconductors that scientists must overcome is their brittleness. The regular, repeating arrangement of the atoms in their crystalline structure make them difficult to form into useful shapes.

In 1987, researchers at the Argonne National Laboratory in Illinois met this challenge by making the first wire from yttrium-barium-copper oxide that was formed into a flexible shape. The wire they produced can be formed into the desired shape while it is "green" or before it is baked to make it superconducting. However, once the wire is fired or heated, it becomes too brittle to bend.

Researchers at International Business Machines have been working on ways to create a new kind of magnetic shield and a new kind of computer wiring. They use a method called *plasma spraying*. Large surfaces of almost any shape are sprayed with superconducting material while the material is still "green." Then the coated surface is heated to thousands of degrees. After gradual cooling, the coating becomes superconducting.

New progress has also been made in manufacturing superconductors so that they are better suited for use in power lines, magnets, and motors. The materials used for these larger applications are made of randomly arranged crystals. For this reason, a portion of the current that passes through them is lost.

By refining the way superconductors are processed, the crystals can be more evenly arranged. When current passes through the superconductor, less of it is lost. The new superconductors now can carry ten times more current than was possible just twelve months ago.

In 1989, scientists at American Telephone and Telegraph Company bombarded a superconductor with neutrons and found that it would then carry 100 times more current than before the treatment.

A NATIONAL EFFORT

In July of 1987, a two-day national conference on superconductivity was held in Washington, D.C. The keynote speaker was President Ronald Reagan. The President announced an eleven-point plan to boost superconductivity research in America. One of the things he asked was that federal funds be increased in the area of superconductivity research.

President Reagan also proposed the formation of a special advisory committee on superconductivity. Since the conference, the committee has advised that American businesses, colleges and universities, and the United States government work together to shorten the time it will take to develop new products using superconductors.

The first joint effort is among IBM, AT&T, Massachusetts Institute of Technology, and Lincoln Laboratory. They will cooperate to develop superconducting electronic devices.

Efforts are being made to further research on superconductors in many other countries as well. These include England, France, Germany, Russia, Japan, India, and China.

INSPIRATION

Superconductivity is an exciting frontier of science. It may be many

Superconducting ceramic shaped into a wire and held by a white-gloved scientist

President Reagan on July 22, 1987, being briefed about superconductivity by leading scientists

years before some of the proposed applications of superconductivity exist. Nevertheless, superconductivity promises to affect our lives in ways we cannot yet imagine.

One unanticipated benefit already is being realized in science classrooms throughout the world. Thousands of students in many countries have already made and tested their own 1-2-3 superconductors. In addition, superconductivity kits available for use in classrooms are being used to demonstrate the Meissner effect.

Superconductivity has fueled a renewed interest in many young people to study science. Perhaps some of them, mesmerized by the sight of a magnet mysteriously hovering above a superconductor of their own making, will be the pioneers who work to answer the questions and meet the challenges that still remain about superconductivity.

President Reagan watching a demonstration of superconducting wire at the Federal Conference on the Commercial Applications of Superconductivity

ACKNOWLEDGMENTS

My sincere appreciation to everyone who has shared their knowledge about superconductivity with me and provided information and photographs for this book. Special thanks to Dr. Paul M. Grant of the IBM Almaden Research Center for reading the manuscript, making suggestions to improve it, and giving permission to use a photograph of his daughter, Heidi, in the book.

Thank you also to Dr. Jay F. Benesch of the Department of Energy for providing drawings and photographs of superconducting magnets and suggesting additional sources of information. Thank you as well to Richard Merwin, Chairman, Eriez Magnetics, and Garry R. Morrow, Vice President, Magstream, Intermagnetics General Corporation, for talking with me about magnetic separators, supplying photographs and information, and offering to be of further assistance. My appreciation, too, to William Austin of General Electric Research and Development Center, who provided valuable information about medical applications of superconductivity as well as photographs to illustrate the book.

Index